For William Caspar Newell – MM

For Jasmine, with love – AC

DIAL BOOKS FOR YOUNG READERS
A division of Penguin Young Readers Group
Published by The Penguin Group
Penguin Group (USA) Inc., 375 Hudson Street, New York, NY 10014, U.S.A.
Penguin Group (Canada), 90 Eglinton Avenue East, Suite 700, Toronto, Ontario, Canada M4P 2Y3 (a division of Pearson Penguin Canada Inc.)
Penguin Books Ltd, 80 Strand, London WC2R 0RL, England
Penguin Ireland, 25 St. Stephen's Green, Dublin 2, Ireland (a division of Penguin Books Ltd)
Penguin Group (Australia), 250 Camberwell Road, Camberwell, Victoria 3124, Australia (a division of Pearson Australia Group Pty Ltd)
Penguin Books India Pvt Ltd, 11 Community Centre, Panchsheel Park, New Delhi - 110 017, India
Penguin Group (NZ), Cnr Airborne and Rosedale Roads, Albany, Auckland 1310, New Zealand (a division of Pearson New Zealand Ltd)
Penguin Books (South Africa) (Pty) Ltd, 24 Sturdee Avenue, Rosebank, Johannesburg 2196, South Africa
Penguin Books Ltd, Registered Offices: 80 Strand, London WC2R 0RL, England

Published in Great Britain 2007 by
Macmillan Children's Books as *Bedtime for Billy Bear*

Published in the United States 2008 by
Dial Books for Young Readers

Text copyright © 2007 by Miriam Moss
Illustrations copyright © 2007 by Anna Currey
All rights reserved
The publisher does not have any control over and does not assume any responsibility for author or third-party websites or their content.

Printed in Belgium
1 3 5 7 9 10 8 6 4 2

Library of Congress Cataloging-in-Publication Data is available upon request.

A Babysitter
for Billy Bear

MIRIAM MOSS
Illustrated by ANNA CURREY

DIAL BOOKS FOR YOUNG READERS

When Billy and Rabbit splashed in from the garden,
Mama and her friend Lucy were having a cup of coffee.

"Oh, just look at you, Billy!" cried Mama.
"You're completely covered in mud!"

Billy looked down at his pants.
"Yes," he said, "and look! So is Rabbit!"
"I think it's time for a bath," said Mama.

Mama washed Billy,
and Billy washed Rabbit.

"Billy," said Mama, "have you remembered that Lucy is looking after you tonight while I go to my pottery class?"

"Yes, I remembered," said Billy,
"but Rabbit forgot."

Mama helped Billy into his pajamas.
"Billy," she said, smiling, "are you looking where
you're putting your feet?"

"I was," said Billy, "but I've lost Rabbit. Where is she?"

"Look, she's over there," said Mama, "drying out after her bath.
She can keep drying downstairs while you
have your snack."

Billy showed Lucy his new pajamas when he got downstairs.

"Oh, they're lovely, Billy," said Lucy.

"Rabbit chose them," said Billy.

"Have you ever had a babysitter before?" Lucy asked Billy.

"No," Billy said. "You're my first. And Rabbit's too."

After his snack, Billy went to find Rabbit.

Billy yawned.

"Rabbit's very tired, you know," he said.

"Yes," said Mama, "I can see that. Come on, up we go!"

Mama helped Billy brush his teeth.
"You have to look this way, Billy," said Mama.
"I can't," said Billy. "Rabbit's fidgeting.
I think something's bothering her."

"What could that be?" asked Mama.
"She wants to go to the pottery class with you," said Billy.

"I'm afraid it's far too late for a young rabbit to be out," said Mama. "But I could make something for her."

Mama read Billy a story and then kissed him good night.
"You've forgotten to sing our song," said Billy.

"I need to go now," said Mama.
"But here's Lucy. She's going to sing with you tonight."
Mama tucked Billy in.
"Good night, Billy. Sleep tight!" she said.

"Lucy, can we sing a noisy song?" Billy asked.
"Of course we can," said Lucy.

After the noisy song, she kissed Billy.
Then, as she went downstairs, he heard her singing
a soft going-to-sleep song.

Silence poured into Billy's room.
"Lucy!" called Billy.
"You forgot to kiss Rabbit."

Lucy came back. She kissed Rabbit
and then kissed Billy again.
"Now close your eyes and go to sleep,"
she said, and left.

Billy closed his eyes,
but he just couldn't sleep.

He climbed out of bed and sat on the stairs.

"What are you doing, Billy?" asked Lucy.
"Rabbit's worried because there's a funny noise
in my room," he said.

Lucy came back upstairs to listen to the noise.
"That's just the wind blowing in the chimney," said Lucy.
"Oh," said Billy.
Lucy tucked him back into bed.

Billy peered over his covers into the corner of the room
where all the dark collected. He didn't like it one bit.

He grabbed Rabbit, jumped out of bed,
and hurried downstairs.

"Rabbit can't get to sleep," said Billy.

"Billy," said Lucy, "if Rabbit is going to be naughty and keep you awake, I'm afraid she's going to have to sleep somewhere else."

Billy's eyes grew wide.

"I don't think she'll like that," he said.

"Well then, you'd better tell her to behave."
Billy's eyes filled with tears.

Lucy lifted Billy gently onto her knee.
"What's the matter, Billy?" she asked.
"It's the dark," said Billy. "Mama won't be able
to find her way home in all the dark."

Lucy took Billy over to the window.

"Look how the moon and stars light up the garden," she said.

"And look at the street lights. Mama will definitely
be able to find her way home."

Billy nodded.

"Should we go upstairs now?" asked Lucy.

"We don't want Mama to come back and find you still up, do we?"

"No," sighed Billy, closing his eyes.

Slowly, Lucy carried Billy back upstairs.

And by the time Mama got home
with Rabbit's pottery present,

Billy was fast asleep.